This Preston Pig Story

Belongs To:

. . . .

For Denise and Klaus

This paperback edition
first published in 2007
by Andersen Press Ltd.
First published in Great Britain in 1994 by
Andersen Press Ltd., 20 Vauxhall Bridge Road, London SW1V 2SA.
Published in Australia by Random House Australia Pty.,
Level 3, 100 Pacific Highway, North Sydney, NSW 2060.
Copyright © Colin McNaughton, 1994
The rights of Colin McNaughton to be identified as the author
and illustrator of this work have been asserted by him in
accordance with the Copyright, Designs and Patents Act, 1988.
All rights reserved.

Colour separated in Switzerland by Photolitho AG, Zürich.
Printed and bound in Singapore.

10   9   8   7   6   5

British Library Cataloguing in Publication Data available.

ISBN 978 1 84270 621 3

This book has been printed on acid-free paper

Suddenly!

A Preston Pig Story

Colin McNaughton

Andersen Press

Preston was walking home
from school one day when
suddenly!

Preston remembered
his mum had asked
him to go to the shops.

Preston was doing
the shopping when

suddenly!

He dashed out of the
shop! (He remembered
he had left the shopping
money in his school desk.)

Preston collected the
money from his desk
and was coming out
of the school when

suddenly!

Preston decided to use
the back door.

On his way back to the shop
Preston stopped at the park
to have a little play when

suddenly!

Billy the bully
shoved past him
and went down the slide!

Preston climbed down
from the slide and went
to do the shopping.
He was just coming out
of the shop when

suddenly!

Mr Plimp the shopkeeper called Preston back to say he had forgotten his change.

At last Preston arrived
home. "Mum," he said.
"I've had the strangest
feeling that someone
has been following me."

suddenly!

Preston's Mum turned around
and gave him an enormous
cuddle!

nee-naa-nee-naa-nee-naa-nee-naa

WOLF HOSPITAL →

Look out!

for the other Preston Pig stories:

www.andersenpress.co.uk